P9-DOG-421

For _____

from _____

with fondest good wishes

for a blessed and heartfelt

Christmastide

The MITFORD SNOWMEN

JAN KARON

The MITFORD SNOWMEN

A Christmas Story

VIKING

VIKING

Published by the Penguin Group

Penguin Putnam Inc., 375 Hudson Street, New York, New York 10014, U.S.A.

Penguin Books Ltd, 27 Wrights Lane, London W8 5TZ, England

Penguin Books Australia Ltd, Ringwood, Victoria, Australia

Penguin Books Canada Ltd, 10 Alcorn Avenue, Toronto, Ontario, Canada M4V 3B2

Penguin Books (N.Z.) Ltd, 182-190 Wairau Road, Auckland 10, New Zealand

Penguin Books Ltd, Registered Offices:
Harmondsworth, Middlesex, England

First published in 2001 by Viking Penguin,
a member of Penguin Putnam Inc.

1 3 5 7 9 10 8 6 4 2

CIP data available.

ISBN: 0-670-03019-8

This book is printed on acid-free paper. ∞

Printed in Mexico
Set in Kennerly
Designed by Francesca Belanger

With warmest thanks
to the very talented
Gary Head and Mary Ann Odom

A T TWO-THIRTY, Mitford's Main Street Grill had fed the breakfast and lunch crowds and was officially closed. However, due to pressing business, three regulars and owner Percy Mosely were still hanging around.

"Four inches an' more comin'!" announced Percy, who was waiting for a sausage delivery from down the mountain. He squinted through the steamy front window at the swirling snowfall. The flakes were large and powdery, reminding him of when he was a kid living in Piney Cove.

"I'm goin' to step out a minute," he said, grabbing his green jacket. "If th' phone rings, call me."

Father Tim Kavanagh, J. C. Hogan, and Mule Skinner would have been glad to get back to work, or even knock off early and go home, but the mayor had recruited them as an advisory committee on the expansion of downtown parking, and their report was due tomorrow.

J.C., the editor of the *Mitford Muse,* wiped his face with a paper napkin. He was sweating this one; he'd never been on an advisory committee before and he wanted to think smart and look good. It wasn't every day that a newspaper editor had a chance to be splashed across his own front page.

"The ballpark is the *only* answer," said J.C. "Given its central location on Main Street, it'd bring traffic in from th' whole county. Besides, it's crazy to blow off retail dollars to maintain a hokey little ball-park."

"*Hokey?*" said Father Tim.

"You leave th' ballpark alone!" Mule felt his blood pressure shooting through the roof. "I don't want to hear ballpark again in this dadgum conversation!"

"Stop acting like a bunch of old women!" said J.C. "We can always get land for another ballpark, but we'll never get another chance like this for downtown parking. It's time to expand our infrastructure."

"*Infrastructure?*" said Mule. "Gag me with a forklift. Where's Percy? Percy's th' oldest business on th' street and do you think he'd go for tearin' down th' ballpark to get a few more warm bodies in here? Nossir, and nobody else will, either."

Mule got up and sprinted to the door, opening it to a blast of cold air.

"Percy! Can you step in here a minute?"

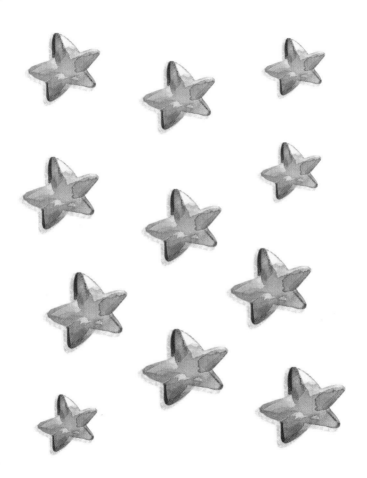

"Tell 'em I'll call back!" Percy was hunkered down at the edge of the sidewalk, building a snowman. "Come out here and help me knock this thing out, there's a contest on th' street!"

Mule looked south on Main Street. Somebody was working on a snowman in front of the Collar Button, and down at Winnie Ivey's Sweet Stuff Bakery there was a whole hive of activity. He peered at Happy Endings Bookstore next door and saw Hope Winchester rolling out the midsection of a snowman as if her life depended on it.

Mule shivered in his knit golf shirt. "Is there a prize in this contest?"

"Somebody said maybe a snow shovel from th' hardware an' a dozen doughnuts from Winnie's."

"Split th' doughnuts and I'll give you a hand."

"Step on it!" said Percy. "An' get th' father an' J.C. out here."

Uncle Billy Watson slogged to the Grill with his pant legs stuffed into his galoshes and his wife's felt hat jammed onto his head. He also wore gloves with both thumbs missing; under an ancient coat of his own, Rose's deceased brother's military jacket displayed a variety of tarnished war medals.

"I was hopin' you'd have a loaf of bread a feller could take home," the old man told Percy. Uncle Billy's arthritic fingers clutched three dimes, a nickel, and two pennies, which he thought was a fair price. "I'll pay cash money, don't you know."

"Go on in an' take it offa th' shelf," said Percy. To tell the truth, he was tired of Bill Watson gouging a loaf of bread out of him every week for the last hundred years, but he wouldn't fret over it now, being the time of year it was.

"What y'uns doin'?" asked Uncle Billy.

Father Tim scooped another shovelful of snow. "There's a snowman contest on Main Street, and Percy wants to nab the prize for the Grill." He was huffing like a steam engine and had lost feeling in most of his fingers and toes.

Uncle Billy surveyed the creation in front of him. "Only thing is, hit's naked as a jaybird."

"Right," said Father Tim. "Needs two eyes, a nose—you know, the basics."

"Needs a hat is more like it," said Uncle Billy. "What's th' prize?"

"Doughnuts. Maybe a snow shovel, but definitely doughnuts."

"Doughnuts!" said Uncle Billy. "Would that be plain or glazed?"

Mayor Esther Cunningham parked her SUV in front of the post office, pulled on a crocheted hat that was gathering dust in the glove compartment, and marched across the street to Happy Endings. Having noticed that small groups of people were gathered up and down the sidewalk, she intended to investigate the commotion.

"What do you think?" asked a beaming Hope Winchester, flushed and frozen.

"I think it's terrific!" said the mayor, peering at a snowman with a book on its head. "What's its name?"

"Bookworm!"

The mayor stood back and looked again, thoughtful, then foraged in her pocketbook. "If that snow-man's goin' to read, he needs a decent pair of glasses. I was goin' to run Ray's old specs up to Hope House, but see what you can do with these."

"Mayor!" bawled Percy. "Come on over!"

The mayor trotted next door to the Grill. "Why, look here! A whole caboodle of snowmen!" Three snow figures stood proudly in the space between the bench and the newspaper box.

"Who does this 'un look like?" asked Uncle Billy, who was now minus part of his clothes and lacking a hat.

"I hate to say it, but that's Rose Watson made over!"

The old man grinned. "Hit's her spit image!"

"I helped," said Father Tim, feeling proud and modest at the same time.

"An' who d'you think *this* is?" asked Percy.

The mayor squinted at the next snowman. "Let's see, now . . ."

"Here's a clue," said Percy, jerking his thumb toward himself. He wished he could quit grinning like an idiot.

"It was my idea to put the pot on its head," said J.C. "Now lookit! Who's this?"

"Shoot, I'd recognize that face anywhere! It's Bill Sprouse over at First Baptist."

"No ma'm," said Uncle Billy, "hit ain't Preacher Sprouse, hit's J.C., don't you know."

J.C. blew on his red hands. "We figured tree lights were kind of different, a little somethin' to catch the judge's eye."

"Who's th' judge?" asked the mayor, feeling out of the loop. Wasn't this her town? How did these things happen without anybody saying doodley-squat to her? Next thing you knew, they'd be running the place themselves and doing a bum job of it.

"Hope, who's the judge of this thing?" the mayor yelled.

"I don't know," said Hope, adjusting the eyeglasses on her entry. "I saw everybody else doing it, so I thought I would, too."

"Mule, go find out who's the judge!" commanded the mayor. Mule hated how the mayor got her way on nearly everything.

In three minutes, he was back, panting from the workout.

"There's not a judge. People saw everybody else doin' it and that's how it happened. Winnie down at Sweet Stuff, she started it. Somebody asked her to be th' judge, but she didn't want th' responsibility."

"Then I'll be the judge!" boomed the mayor.

"Don't even fool with goin' down th' block," said Uncle Billy. "They ain't no use to judge anybody's but cur'n." He brushed snow off the bench so the mayor could have a seat. "You got your top winners right here."

"As judge of the First Annual Mitford Snowman Jubilee," proclaimed the mayor, "I declare *every* entrant a winner, with free doughnuts and hot chocolate for everybody on the street!"

At the sound of whistles and cheers, she launched two fists into the air with thumbs up, a campaign tactic she'd always favored.

The heck with her penny-pinching council, she thought, storming along in her fleece-lined boots to the Sweet Stuff Bakery. As the happy crowd fell in behind her, she calculated how she'd gouge the money out of the Parks and Recreation Committee. If that failed, she'd find the measly few bucks somewhere; after all, wasn't this her town, and wouldn't such a gesture be good for business in general? She drew herself up proudly as she advanced toward the bakery. Bottom line, didn't Mitford take care of its own?

She was still huffing from her block-and-a-half gallop as the twenty-six people in her wake formed an excited but orderly queue at Sweet Stuff Bakery.

Mule opened the door. "Age after beauty," he said to the mayor. "You go first!"

"I'll do no such thing," she pronounced, grabbing the door and holding it open herself.

Just then, the town Christmas lights switched on at their appointed hour. And suddenly, the whole of Main Street was softly illumined against

the approaching winter dusk; every lamppost glimmered with lights formed in the shape of angels, their wings outspread in the falling snow.

In the window of the bakery, colored bubble lights encircled a nativity scene made of gingerbread and marzipan.

Five-year-old Amy Larkin, who was shopping with her family, stood on tiptoes and peered into the window. "I would never eat the Holy Family," she said in a hushed voice.

"I would eat a camel or maybe a donkey!" declared her cousin.

As the crowd rushed in through the open door, the fragrance of cinnamon and chocolate rushed out.

"Merry Christmas, everybody!"

"Merry Christmas, Mayor!"

Uncle Billy's gold tooth flashed in a smile that

seemed to take over his entire face. He would hope for a marshmallow in his hot chocolate, but he wouldn't ask. He'd save the asking for an extra doughnut to carry home to Rose. After all, it was Christmas.

Hallmark offers a wide selection of Mitford
home décor and gift items, including products that feature
the charming Mitford snowmen found in this book.
For more information about Hallmark products,
call 1-800-HALLMARK, or visit us at
www.hallmark.com.